Inana

by Michele Lowe

A SAMUEL FRENCH ACTING EDITION

FOUNDED 1830

NEW YORK HOLLYWOOD LONDON TORONTO

SAMUELFRENCH.COM

ISBN 978-0-573-69917-7   Printed in U.S.A.   #29803

MUSIC USE NOTE

IMPORTANT BILLING AND CREDIT
REQUIREMENTS

INANA was first produced by the Denver Center Theatre in Denver, Colorado on January 22, 2009. The performance was directed by Michael Pressman, with sets by Vicki Smith, costumes by David Kay Mickelsen, lighting by Ann G. Wrightson, sound by Morgan McCauley, music by Lindsay Jones, and dramaturgy by Douglas Langworthy. The production stage manager was Phoebe Sacks. The production assistant was Rick Noble. The cast was as follows:

YASIN	Piter Marek
SHALI	Mahira Kakkar
WAITER/DOMINIC CROFT	David Ivers
ABDEL-HAKIM TALIQ	Laith Nakli
MOHAMMED/MESSENGER	Alok Tewari
MENA/HAMA	Reema Zaman
EMAD	Nasser Faris

CHARACTERS

YASIN SHALID – an Iraqi, chief of the Mosul Museum

SHALI SHALID – his Iraqi bride

WAITER – a British man

ABDEL-HAKIM TALIQ – an Iraqi bookseller

MOHAMMED ZARA – an Iraqi, assistant to Yasin

MENA MOHAMMED – Shali's younger sister

HAMA SHALID – Yasin's first wife, doubles with Mena

EMAD AL-BAYIT – Shali's father, an Iraqi artists

DOMINIC CROFT – a British curator of the British Museum, doubles with Waiter

MESSENGER – an Iraqi man, doubles with Mohammed

SETTING

A hotel room in London.

TIME

February 4, 2003

Dedicated to the people of Iraq,
who watch over the world's legacy
with decency and compassion.

(Late afternoon. A shabby hotel room in London. There is a window on the upstage wall. The furnishings are dingy and worn. Several suitcases are piled near the door that leads to the hotel hallway. The door to the bathroom is stage left. The television is on but there's no sound. **YASIN SHALID**, *dressed in a rumpled suit, glances at it from time to time. He addresses the bathroom door which is closed.)*

YASIN. I've ordered up some tea and a plate of biscuits.

(He waits for a response.)

I take three sugars with my tea.

(No response.)

They make lovely biscuits in London. Very sugary. No nuts. Unless you order them with nuts. I once cracked a tooth on a biscuit in Cairo. I'd gone there for a conference in '98. One of the conservators at the Cairo Museum had a cousin who was a dentist. Saved my life. Then the conservator, I don't remember his name, insisted on taking me to El-Amarna. He was all puffed up like a peacock showing me around but El-Amarna was in terrible shape. The Egyptians don't protect their sites like we do. Anybody can walk right in. I saw one little girl pick up a cylinder and put it in a plastic purse. Nobody said anything. No one stopped her. So off it went – a 4000 year-old antiquity into the hands of an eight year-old girl.

(No response.)

The Egyptian workers don't look particularly intelligent, but they're shrewd. The administrators don't permit them to wear anything with pockets or layers under their clothes, so the guards don't bother looking at them when they leave at night. Nobody pats them down or checks their bags. When I worked in Babylon, nobody left the site unless they were inspected from the inside out. Everyone was suspect, even me. I was insulted at first, but then I saw that it made the men respect me a little more if I submitted to the searches, too. I wasn't one of them, of course, but I was willing to play the part.

(No response.)

YASIN. *(cont.)* When I was a boy, I had a friend, Ralwa, who lived across the alley. We used to go to Nimrud after dark and dig in the ruins. He had the flashlight, I had the trowel. We would find broken tablets, small vessels, little things under the clay and keep them. It was fun just being outside at night and digging, collecting what we could. Then one day Ralwa's uncle found the treasures and turned him over to the police. Ralwa never told his uncle about me. I know because the police never came to our house. Ralwa took his punishment and we never went back. They cut off two of his fingers – the pinky and the third finger on his right hand. When I couldn't go to sleep, I used to lay in bed and imagine what it felt like not to have fingers.

(pause)

Then I heard Ralwa's uncle was going down to Nimrud at night with Ralwa's flashlight.

(Something on the television catches his eye.)

Oh, yes in the back of the net! United are one up!

(pause)

Do you watch football?

(No response.)

Is there something I can get you from out here? I haven't touched your suitcase. My first wife never let me touch any of her things. Said I was an animal on the loose when I opened the bureau.

(No response.)

YASIN. *(cont.)* Is there a showerhead in the tub? I specifically requested a showerhead when I made the reservation. Not all the rooms come with it.

(No response.)

Look, if there's something wrong, I wish you'd tell me. If you're disappointed or alarmed just say so. I won't be angry.

(No response.)

Would you at least run some water so I know you're all right.

(Silence. The sound of running water from the bathroom. The water is shut off.)

(A knock at the hallway door.)

Who's there?

WAITER *(offstage)* Room service.

YASIN. *(to the bathroom door)* Tea's here.

(YASIN opens the door to the hall. A **WAITER** *enters holding a tray.)*

WAITER. Sorry it took so long. There's a mini-conference downstairs. Damn Norwegians and their fucking snow removal systems. I stood in the back and listened till I thought I was going to blow my fucking brains out.

YASIN. I'll take it, thank you. Have there been any calls for me?

WAITER. A calls comes in, we send it right up. You sure you don't want me to lay out the tea?

YASIN. No, that's fine.

WAITER. It's included in the service.

YASIN. Thank you, no.

WAITER. Kitchen closes in half an hour.

YASIN. Are there any restaurants?

WAITER. It's Sunday. Everything closes at four. It's like they roll up the fucking red carpet.

YASIN. There's a lady present.

(**YASIN** *indicates the bathroom.*)

WAITER. *(to bathroom door)* Begging your pardon.

> *(to* **YASIN***)*

> Been watching too much of the matches. Dial 42 when you want me to pick up the tray.

(**YASIN** *pulls him aside.*)

YASIN. Did you see the Manchester game?

WAITER. Beckham's goal was an absolute cracker. My money's on them to win the league.

YASIN. I'd love to see them stuff Arsenal.

WAITER. Me, too.

> *(to bathroom door)*

> 'Night, Ma'am!

> *(to* **YASIN***)*

> Come on you Reds! Huzzah!

> *(He exits.)*

YASIN. *(to the bathroom door)* Are you going to pour tea?

> *(No response.)*

> *(Lights up inside the bathroom.* **SHALI** *sits on the edge of the tub. She is dressed in a white coat with matching white satin gloves that reach up to her elbow.)*

They've given us several kinds. Isn't that lucky?

SHALI. Is there plain tea?

YASIN. I'm sure there's something mild.

SHALI. I prefer plain.

YASIN. Yes, there's Darjeeling.

SHALI. Is that what we get at home?

YASIN. Similar.

SHALI. Plain?

YASIN. Yes.

SHALI. I might like that.

> *(beat)*

YASIN. Hot tea would be good right about now, don't you think?

(She doesn't respond.)

I've selected a poem in honor of today. I don't usually have the stomach for Rumi, I find him excessive. My first wife asked me to write an original poem for our wedding and I don't think she was pleased with my efforts. So I decided to use a professional this time.

(He pulls a wrinkled piece of paper out of his suit jacket.)

(reading)

"This marriage be wine with halvah
Honey dissolving in milk.

This marriage be the leaves and fruit of a date tree.
This marriage

be women laughing together for days
on end. This marriage, a sign

for us to study.
This marriage beauty. A moon

in a light blue sky. This marriage,
this silence, fully mixed with spirit."

SHALI. The middle lines – the ones about study – ?

YASIN. "…This marriage, a sign for us to study."

SHALI. I like those. What's it called?

YASIN. Oh yes, the title: "Blessed Marriage."

(No response.)

Were there any other lines that appealed to you?

SHALI. I'm sorry, I can't remember them.

(beat)

YASIN. Would you like me to read it again?

SHALI. Yasin?

YASIN. Yes?

SHALI. Why did we have to leave?

YASIN. *(lying)* We didn't *have* to.

SHALI. Then why did we come here?

YASIN. Come into the room and I'll tell you.

SHALI. Who is McGuire Gibson?

(**YASIN** *doesn't respond.*)

You spoke to him when we arrived.

YASIN. He lives in America. He asked me to call.

SHALI. Why?

YASIN. I think he wanted to congratulate us on our marriage.

SHALI. You said, "We're home," to Mr. Gibson.

YASIN. Did I?

SHALI. Yes. You said, "We're home."

YASIN. I don't think I meant –

SHALI. *(overlapping)* You meant that we're in our temporary home. Because we're very far from where we live.

(**YASIN** *looks out the window.*)

YASIN. The sun is sinking over the little park and it's very beautiful right now.

(*The bathroom door opens.*)

SHALI. Is it still there?

YASIN. The sun?

SHALI. The beautiful.

YASIN. Yes, in front of the hotel.

(**SHALI** *enters the bedroom.*)

"She comes to me in wedding white,
under moon and starry night."

SHALI. Is that also Rumi?

YASIN. No.

SHALI. Did you write it for your first wife?

(*No response.*)

I like it. I like it much more than Rumi's poem. You are the true poet.

YASIN. I'm truly not.

SHALI. Please tell me the rest.

YASIN. I don't remember.

SHALI. Say those lines again, then.

YASIN. *(gently)* They've gone out of my head.

> (**SHALI** *glances out the window and says nothing.*)
>
> *(She pours tea.)*

SHALI. *(remembering)* Three sugars.

YASIN. Tomorrow we can walk the park if you like.

SHALI. Can't we go now?

YASIN. I'm expecting a telephone call.

SHALI. From Mr. Gibson?

YASIN. No, from someone here in London. Someone from the British Museum.

> *(She moves toward the bathroom.)*

Where are you – ?

SHALI. *(overlapping)* The plate's dirty.

> *(She exits into the bathroom. The door remains open as she washes the dish.)*
>
> *(offstage)*

I don't understand how people serve food on filthy plates.

YASIN. I'm sure it doesn't happen often.

SHALI *(offstage)* Do you like London?

YASIN. Don't you?

SHALI *(offstage)* It's dirty.

YASIN. You've barely seen it.

SHALI *(offstage)* I saw the airport.

YASIN. You think London's dirtier than Mosul?

> *(She enters.)*

SHALI. Mosul isn't dirty.

YASIN. It's dusty and drab and decaying.

SHALI. I thought men like you liked decay.

YASIN. Like me?

SHALI. Men who dig in the ruins.

YASIN. That doesn't mean I like decay. The last thing I want is –

SHALI. *(overlapping)* What's the first thing you want?

(beat)

YASIN. Carefully preserved objects of antiquity.

SHALI. Are there such things?

YASIN. Rarely.

SHALI. Did you find any in Babylon?

YASIN. I found a cuneiform tablet. Part of the Babylon Chronicle. I put the date at 600 BCE.

SHALI. Did it make you famous?

YASIN. I wrote a paper about it. People read it.

SHALI. Did you keep it?

YASIN. The tablet? No, I put it in the Mosul museum: third floor, second case on the left, number 683.

SHALI. I've never been to your museum. My father wouldn't allow it.

YASIN. It isn't *my* museum.

SHALI. My father said you're the chief. That's why we can't stay very long, can we? We're on our wedding trip.

(He takes a picture out of his wallet and shows it to her.)

YASIN. That's the tablet.

SHALI. I thought it would be bigger.

YASIN. Yes it's small, but it's intact. That's unusual.

SHALI. And you say it's important?

YASIN. It outlines the wars between the Assyrians and the Egyptians. It's very detailed. One of a kind.

SHALI. I look forward to seeing it. When we return to Mosul you can show it to me.

(silence)

Why didn't the Egyptian guards at El-Amarna arrest the workers if they knew they were stealing?

YASIN. They were all related.

SHALI. I don't understand.

YASIN. Each of the Egyptian workers came from the same tribe of at least one of the guards. If they'd pointed fingers at each other it would have been chaos. Everyone would have lost their jobs. Besides, I'm sure the workers cut the guards in on what they sold.

SHALI. Did they ever catch Ralwa's uncle?

YASIN. Stealing? No. But I heard later that he was part of a pipeline to America.

SHALI. Did Ralwa ever talk about his missing fingers?

YASIN. I never asked.

SHALI. You never asked him about his chopped off fingers?

YASIN. I didn't think he'd want to talk about it.

SHALI. Oh, you should have asked him. He would have told you that Saddam keeps them. All the little ears and fingers and lengths of arm and leg go into massive refrigerators in a hospital outside of Samarra.

YASIN. You're joking.

SHALI. I'm not joking at all.

YASIN. Shali, they get tossed in the trash.

SHALI. No, Yasin, you're mistaken. There are several dozen doctors whose sole job is to maintain everything that's been severed. It's true, I swear it. I've seen pictures of the hospital.

YASIN. Pictures?

SHALI. Absolutely. And I met a doctor who works there, a friend of my father's. He says it's a wonderful place. Everything there is pink and healthy.

YASIN. How could they possibly keep and identify all of the pieces?

SHALI. Isn't that what you do? Keep track of all the little pieces? Little pieces discarded by time. You do it, why not Saddam? I have a cousin whose arm was cut off because she was too beautiful. They assured her that if she was a very good girl they would give it back to her someday. They said that Saddam was always watching all the children to make sure they were being good. Ask Ralwa the next time you see him. He knows all about the refrigerators.

YASIN. Ralwa disappeared many years ago. He and my brother Manhal were taken to the desert.

SHALI. God be with them. My cousin Yusuf was taken ten years ago.

YASIN. God bless him, too.

(**SHALI**'s attention is drawn to the TV.)

SHALI. He looked like that man on TV.

(**YASIN** looks.)

YASIN. That man works for the American president. His name is Colin Powell. He's like one of our ministers. He's going to make a speech before the UN tomorrow.

SHALI. What will he say?

YASIN. That we are a threat to the world.

SHALI. Do the Americans really fear us? Do they really think we're that capable?

YASIN. So they say.

SHALI. They give us too much credit.

(beat)

YASIN. (intrigued) You're very smart, aren't you?

SHALI. I'm only as smart you want me to be.

YASIN. How did you learn to read?

SHALI. My older sister, Luma, went to school before they closed it. She taught me.

YASIN. And you're eighteen.

SHALI. Is that disappointing to you? Did you want a younger wife?

YASIN. I didn't want any wife.

SHALI. Until?

YASIN. Until I met your father, of course.

SHALI. Does he know where I am?

YASIN. No. No one knows.

SHALI. When may I tell my father where I am?

YASIN. You can call him right now. But do it quickly.

(He dials his mobile phone and hands it to her. She listens.)

SHALI. He's not answering.

YASIN. He's probably asleep.

SHALI. More likely he's still celebrating. My father enjoys marrying off his daughters. Was our wedding different from your first?

YASIN. All weddings are different from each other.

SHALI. Even if some of the people are the same?

(YASIN doesn't respond.)

May I call my family again in the morning?

YASIN. You can try before I leave, then I'll need my phone. I'll be gone most of the day.

SHALI. I don't understand.

YASIN. You can stay here and watch TV. I'm sure there'll be more news.

SHALI. Can't I go with you?

YASIN. Out of the question.

SHALI. But I've never –

YASIN. *(overlapping)* You'll be perfectly safe.

SHALI. No one's ever left me alone.

YASIN. There's nothing to be –

SHALI. *(overlapping)* Couldn't you put me somewhere else? Some place I'm not by myself?

YASIN. There is no other place.

SHALI. What if you don't come back? What if you decide in the morning that you don't like me and you go to Damascus or Tehran?

YASIN. I'm going to the British Museum.

SHALI. But the person from the British Museum hasn't called.

YASIN. He will.

SHALI. How do you know?

YASIN. Because he knew I was coming today.

SHALI. If you leave me here I'll die. I'll die right here in this room.

YASIN. You're acting like a little girl.

SHALI. Because I *am*. I told you I'm only –

(She stops short.)

YASIN. You're only what?

SHALI. Young.

YASIN. How old are you really? You're not 18. I know that.

SHALI. I'm merely 23, my king.

YASIN. Your father told me you were –

SHALI. Don't be angry with my father. He's so old he doesn't remember. Some days I'm 23, other days 18. But I read and I write quite well. I can write a letter for you to Mr. Gibson.

YASIN. I don't need to write –

SHALI. I have paper in my bag –

(To get to her bag, she must first move a large red suitcase.)

YASIN. *(angrily)* Keep off that red suitcase!

SHALI. I just need my –

YASIN. I don't need to write a letter and if I did, I'd write it myself.

SHALI. May I have my bag, please? Thank you.

YASIN. *(covering)* The red suitcase is quite heavy. I wouldn't want you to hurt yourself.

SHALI. I once lifted a suitcase and carried it three kilometers for my Aunt. That suitcase was also red, not that particular red, it had more orange in it. There are ninety-two reds. Blood itself comes in twenty four shades.

YASIN. The deeper the cut, the darker the red.

SHALI. When I was little, my father bought me art books from a bookseller in Bakir. I still have them at home.

YASIN. He bought them from Abdel-Hakim Taliq.

SHALI. I don't remember his name.

YASIN. His family has sold books for six generations; Egyptian cookbooks, Iranian atlases, old Turkish love stories. He keeps the first Iraqi edition of *Hamlet* locked in a little case behind his desk and wears the key around his neck.

ABDEL-HAKIM. *(offstage) (in pain)* AWWWWW!

YASIN. And they hated him for it. They tortured him.

ABDEL-HAKIM. *(offstage)* AWWWW!

(Lights down on hotel room.)

(Music. **YASIN** *remembers visiting the bookshop in Bakir. He becomes immersed in the memory.)*

YASIN. Where are you, Abdel-Hakim? Why are all the lights out? Yes, I saw them leaving they're down the block; they're watching to see what you'll do. What did you display in the window? You mock them. You mock them and they know it. The neighborhood knows it. Probably the whole country knows it by now.

*(***ABDEL-HAKIM** *enters with his bleeding hand wrapped in dirty towel.)*

ABDEL-HAKIM. It wasn't even a picture – it was a *drawing*!

YASIN. A pencil drawing?

ABDEL-HAKIM. A charcoal drawing of a baby – a *human* baby.

YASIN. Was it naked?

ABDEL-HAKIM. Owwww.

YASIN. Was it?

ABDEL-HAKIM. It was study for one of Titian's angels.

YASIN. *(slightly annoyed)* A voluptuous angel?

ABDEL-HAKIM. Yes, of course.

YASIN. It's your own fault then.

ABDEL-HAKIM. My hand is killing me.

YASIN. Go to the hospital.

ABDEL-HAKIM. It's filthy there.

YASIN. Then let your wife bandage it.

ABDEL-HAKIM. She'll also say it's my fault.

> (**YASIN** *sees* **ABDEL-HAKIM***'s wound.*)

YASIN. Ugh.

ABDEL-HAKIM. Will they grow back?

YASIN. I don't know. You'll have to look in one of your medical textbooks.

ABDEL-HAKIM. Look for me will you, Yasin?

> (**ABDEL-HAKIM** *indicates a bookcase.*)

Over there.

> (**YASIN** *finds a book.*)

YASIN. "A History of Fourteenth Century Medicine."

ABDEL-HAKIM. An abundance of curatives known to give little comfort.

YASIN. "Salves and Dressings as described by the Eternal."

ABDEL-HAKIM. Ancient and incomprehensible but the drawings are museum quality.

YASIN. *(ironically)* Perhaps you have something more current?

ABDEL-HAKIM. Not up here. Oh, Yasin it burns and it itches and then it throbs.

YASIN. You should lock up and go home.

ABDEL-HAKIM. I'd rather bleed to death.

YASIN. I'm sure they wouldn't mind.

ABDEL-HAKIM. What is it you came for?

YASIN. It can wait.

ABDEL-HAKIM. Tell me, tell me. It'll take my mind off the pain.

YASIN. A book by John Curtis.

ABDEL-HAKIM. I don't have it.

YASIN. *(pressing on)* It's called "Recent Excavations by the British Museum."

ABDEL-HAKIM. I know all of my books, all of my authors. John Curtis isn't here.

YASIN. What about downstairs?

ABDEL-HAKIM. Ssssht! *No.*

YASIN. Can you get it for me, my friend?

ABDEL-HAKIM. Are there any naked people in it?

YASIN. It's about a dig in Chechnya.

ABDEL-HAKIM. It's still possible.

YASIN. I'm sure the Chechneians were clothed.

ABDEL-HAKIM. Write down the title and I'll call tomorrow. Unless the pain kills me first.

YASIN. *Go to the hospital.*

ABDEL-HAKIM. It's the second time this week the goons have come. Now every book that contains a picture of *anything* with a heartbeat, even a cockroach, must go into storage or they'll burn it. They ripped up a book I'd ordered for Emad Al-Bayit because it had bees on the cover. Bumble bees!

YASIN. You're working with Emad?

ABDEL-HAKIM. He comes to see me when he's in town.

YASIN. He's a criminal.

ABDEL-HAKIM. He's a good customer. And you can't call him a criminal, he's never been arrested.

YASIN. Neither have the men who mangled your hand. You place a book of God's creatures on your shelf and get your nails torn out. Emad forges dozens of antiquities and gets away with it every time. Where's the justice in that?

ABDEL-HAKIM. *(quietly)* I'll tell you what I told Emad: I'm clearing out. I'm moving all the books in my basement to Tehran.

YASIN. How many?

ABDEL-HAKIM. Fifty thousand. Maybe more.

YASIN. Impossible.

ABDEL-HAKIM. "How poor are they that have not patience! What wound did ever heal but by degrees?"

YASIN. Patience or not it can't be done.

ABDEL-HAKIM. Yesterday, I sent one of my men over the border wearing a coat with sixteen books sewn into the lining.

YASIN. At that rate you'll be finished in forty years.

ABDEL-HAKIM. With the help of God, maybe a year or two less. But I am determined! I'm building a library there. I'll have a bookshop, too. I have a cousin there who can run it for me.

YASIN. You won't go?

ABDEL-HAKIM. I was born to die here.

YASIN. Not to be with your books?

ABDEL-HAKIM. I'll visit them.

YASIN. But what'll you do once they're all gone?

ABDEL-HAKIM. Collect more to send. What can I do? If the Americans invade I could lose them all.

YASIN. We've started packing crates to send to Baghdad.

ABDEL-HAKIM. God protect us from another war. Don't you have storage space here?

YASIN. Not enough. They have vaults in the National Museum – steel lined, deep in the ground. The objects will be safe there, and what we can't move we'll protect as best we can.

ABDEL-HAKIM. "The worst is not

So long as we can say, 'This is the worst.'"

(off his bloody hand)

You should get the apes who did this to me to guard your museum.

YASIN. I'll tell you what concerns me most.

(Lights up on a statue of a woman three feet high. She is naked and missing her left arm from the shoulder down. She is visible only to **YASIN.***)*

ABDEL-HAKIM. Your statue.

YASIN. *Inana.*

ABDEL-HAKIM. The one armed goddess.

YASIN. Rassam searched for her arm for two years before he gave up.

ABDEL-HAKIM. Goddess of War.

YASIN. She is too beautiful.

ABDEL-HAKIM. Goddess of Sex.

YASIN. She needs me.

ABDEL-HAKIM. Any woman who has been around for 3000 years needs little help from you.

YASIN. Provocative, handsome, glorious and yet –

ABDEL-HAKIM. Stone.

YASIN. Fragile.

ABDEL-HAKIM. Damaged.

YASIN. Exquisite.

ABDEL-HAKIM. You need a wife.

YASIN. I had a wife.

(Lights down on the statue.)

ABDEL-HAKIM. A new one. People wonder why you don't remarry.

YASIN. Tell them I'm too busy packing.

ABDEL-HAKIM. Not for five years.

YASIN. Tell them I'm too busy protecting the heritage of our country, our patrimony, the world's legacy…

ABDEL-HAKIM. I have a cousin in Tahreer; he has a daughter. I've never seen her, but I could inquire about her.

YASIN. Could I keep the goddess here in your basement?

ABDEL-HAKIM. Here?

YASIN. If I sent her to the National there's no guarantee I'd get her back.

ABDEL-HAKIM. But Inana is yours.

YASIN. I've been avoiding the curators there for years. Whenever they asked me to loan them Inana I'd make

up some excuse about an exhibition here. Two weeks
ago they sent me a letter demanding that I send her to
them for safekeeping.

ABDEL-HAKIM. It would only be temporary.

YASIN. They would absolutely try to keep her.

ABDEL-HAKIM. Don't you have any friends there?

YASIN. All of my friends would love to get their hands on
her.

ABDEL-HAKIM. Yes, but if you don't send the statue to
Baghdad and something happens to it –

YASIN. *(overlapping)* Nothing's going to happen. Especially
if she's here.

ABDEL-HAKIM. It isn't safe. The goons will be back.

YASIN. No one but us would know.

ABDEL-HAKIM. The walls have ears. And she's naked, isn't
she?

YASIN. It's not the same.

ABDEL-HAKIM. You want her in pieces? Like the glass in the
window? I can't be responsible.

YASIN. I'll take full responsibility.

ABDEL-HAKIM. I'll get you a picture of my cousin's girl.
If she pleases you, we'll put our heads together. But
you'll have to deal with the goddess yourself. Forgive
me –

YASIN. Abdel-Hakim wait –

ABDEL-HAKIM. I'm headed to the hospital.

(**ABDEL-HAKIM** *exits.*)

(**YASIN**'s *memory fades.*)

(*Lights back up on* **SHALI** *in the hotel room.*)

SHALI. Yasin, are you all right?

YASIN. They were calling me twice a day sometimes three
times.

SHALI. Who was?

YASIN. The people at the National Museum. They wanted
me to send them the statue of Inana immediately.

SHALI. The statue of Inana? Why?

YASIN. For safekeeping.

SHALI. Because of the Americans?

YASIN. But she didn't belong in Bagdad. It would have been disaster.

SHALI. You didn't want to send her to a place she didn't belong.

YASIN. Exactly.

SHALI. Where she might feel uncomfortable or strange.

YASIN. Yes.

SHALI. Did you send her?

YASIN. It was a difficult decision.

SHALI. Did the bookseller help you decide?

YASIN. In a roundabout way.

(He elaborates no further.)

SHALI. Could you take me to his shop one day? It's been years since I've seen a new book.

(No response.)

I met your friend Mohammed at the wedding.

YASIN. Mohammed's my assistant.

SHALI. He told me that if the Americans invade, he'll lock himself inside the museum and strap himself to the Balawat Gates. He said he'd never leave. I admire his dedication.

YASIN. Most days everyone arrived at the museum before sun up. If we were too tired to go home at night we slept there. I had cots put into the largest offices. In the last five months, we shipped 400 crates to Baghdad. Anything too heavy to move was covered in foam or sandbagged around it's pedestal. Everything had to be protected.

(Lights down on the hotel room.)

*(Music. Lights up on **MOHAMMED ZARA**, **YASIN**'s assistant, in the courtyard of the Mosul Museum. **YASIN** remembers a particular meeting and joins **MOHAMMED** in the memory.)*

MOHAMMED. Married!

YASIN. Next Sunday.

MOHAMMED. This is wonderful! Have you met her?

YASIN. For an hour.

MOHAMMED. Is she beautiful?

YASIN. Yes, but not too beautiful.

MOHAMMED. God bless you both.

YASIN. After the ceremony we're going on a little wedding trip.

MOHAMMED. You're leaving? Now?

YASIN. While I'm away you'll be in charge.

MOHAMMED. Me?

YASIN. You know everything that goes on here and your English is better than anyone else's. That might come in handy should the Marines arrive.

MOHAMMED. Are you joking?

YASIN. Look at it this way: the Americans aren't party to the '54 Hague. They don't give a damn about protecting antiquities or excavation sites. With all our friends in America, the generals still refuse to guarantee us any kind of protection. So if the Marines do appear at our front door it might mean they've changed their minds. Or not.

MOHAMMED. How long will you be away?

YASIN. I'll phone you the middle of the week.

MOHAMMED. At least tell me where you're going.

YASIN. I can't. It's a surprise for my bride.

MOHAMMED. After all this time, why marry now?

YASIN. Why not now? A man must strike when the iron is hot.

MOHAMMED. The iron has been cool for five years, couldn't you wait a little longer before warming it up?

YASIN. You'll be a fine leader, Mohammed. The staff likes you.

MOHAMMED. They won't like you leaving. They're anxious enough about the Americans.

YASIN. What are they saying?

MOHAMMED. It's what they don't say that gives them away.

YASIN. I don't want nervous fingers packing the cases.

MOHAMMED. No, of course not.

YASIN. And the cataloguing?

MOHAMMED. Coming slowly.

YASIN. Put more people on it.

MOHAMMED. I already have.

YASIN. I need every object photographed and entered into the database.

MOHAMMED. It's being done.

YASIN. Mohammed, one more thing: I need a card for every object on my desk by next Friday.

MOHAMMED. A card?

YASIN. An index card.

MOHAMMED. I'll make a copy of the file for you.

YASIN. I want every object on an individual card, something I can touch and feel.

MOHAMMED. But you never said –

YASIN. *(cutting him short)* I'm adding it to the list.

MOHAMMED. We would need thousands of blank cards.

YASIN. There are 5000 in the stock room.

MOHAMMED. We haven't done that in years. Let me finish updating the database and then we can talk about cards.

YASIN. There's nothing to talk about. I need the cards finished by Friday.

MOHAMMED. But Yasin –

YASIN. *(cutting him short)* Think of them as a wedding gift.

MOHAMMED. Blessings on you both.

(**MOHAMMED** *exits. The memory fades.*)

(*Lights back up on the hotel room.* **YASIN** *joins* **SHALI** *again.*)

YASIN. Mohammed would have been successful earlier in his career, but instead of traveling and attending conferences, he preferred to stay home and read books.

SHALI. Like me.

YASIN. Perhaps your father should have made you a match with him.

SHALI. I was only saying that I enjoyed meeting him.

YASIN. I thought you'd like London. Or at the very least would be grateful to leave Iraq. If the Americans invade –

SHALI. *(overlapping)* God will protect us.

YASIN. It'll be complete chaos.

SHALI. Not if Saddam's men do what they say.

YASIN. America is a superpower, we are a tiny little country! We are a piece of nothing.

SHALI. We are a piece of God.

YASIN. Eight hundred years ago, when the Mongols wiped out Baghdad, they took all the manuscripts in the libraries and tossed them into the Tigris. They say so many books were lost that the river ran black with ink. Now instead of the Mongols, the art collectors are coming. The professionals and the petty thieves all have their eyes on us. They're backing up their trucks, dreaming of their black market fortunes. But when they open the glass cases and reach for our very hearts, they'll come up against forces even they can't fight.

SHALI. You mean Saddam's men?

YASIN. I mean Ralwa. Ralwa and my brother Manhal and your cousin Yusuf and my colleague Abu Ahmed and his neighbor and her father and my uncle – *all of them* – they're all coming back.

SHALI. An army of ghosts? That's who you think will protect us?

YASIN. Some say there are more of them than there are of us.

(There's a knock on the door.)

YASIN. Who's there?

WAITER *(offstage)* Up the Reds! Huzzah!

*(The **WAITER** enters with a heaping tray of food.)*

Courtesy of the Norwegians. Amazing group actually. If you listen long enough they're a convincing bunch. They're talking about one machine that can lift two tons of snow and send it over to Greenland. Not that they need it.

YASIN. I didn't order –

WAITER. *(overlapping)* They said downstairs you'd gotten married this morning. Congratulations.

SHALI. We've been to three countries in one day.

WAITER. Did you rob a bank?

SHALI. No. We were married in Iraq, then drove to Jordan, then flew here.

YASIN. He was making a joke, Shali.

WAITER. Well, welcome to London. Smashing place for a honeymoon. This is for you.

(He places the tray of food in front of them.)

YASIN. We can't accept it.

SHALI. *(to YASIN)* But we haven't eaten.

YASIN. *(to the WAITER)* Thank you very much but –

WAITER. *(overlapping)* Did I do something wrong?

YASIN. I didn't order the food.

WAITER. If it's a matter of money –

YASIN. *(lying, overlapping)* It's not.

WAITER. Think of it as a wedding gift. Straight out of the fridge, we didn't put it out on the buffet. The Norwegians over-ordered that's all.

SHALI. Please, Yasin.

WAITER. Eat what you like and then ring me when you're done. It'll get tossed in the trash if you don't take it.

SHALI. It's all right, isn't it Yasin?

(beat)

YASIN. Pity to throw it all out.

SHALI. *(to* WAITER*)* Thank you very much.

WAITER. The food's on the house but the service isn't.

YASIN. Is someone at the front desk at all times?

WAITER. Yes sir, either myself or Bridget.

YASIN. And on the switchboard?

WAITER. We have Elizabeth. Bridget spots her when she takes her break. You know, goes to the loo, or has her ciggie. You can count on us.

*(*YASIN *finally tips him.)*

Cheers.

(The WAITER *exits.)*

*(*SHALI *unwraps the platter.)*

SHALI. *(off the tray)* Is that fish?

YASIN. Maybe.

(off another part of the tray)

That looks like some kind of vegetable.

SHALI. Carrots?

YASIN. I don't like carrots.

SHALI. Perhaps it's sweet potato.

(She tastes a little.)

SHALI. *(disappointed)* Squash. It hasn't been seasoned, not even with salt. It's quite dull. Is that mutton?

YASIN. I like mutton.

SHALI. It smells bad.

YASIN. I once had bad mutton and would up in the hospital.

SHALI. Dear God.

YASIN. Do you like *kufta?*

SHALI. I make a delicious *kufta* with sweet garlic that my sister Luma grows in her yard.

YASIN. There's a little restaurant here on Kings Street that makes the best *kufta* I've ever had. We can go there if you like.

SHALI. *(unenthusiastic)* If you like.

YASIN. But not tonight. Besides it's after four. All the restaurants are closed.

SHALI. The restaurants in Mosul always stay open late on Sunday.

YASIN. We can go another time.

(*pause*)

Since we have no other plans for the evening –

(He turns off the TV.)

Perhaps we should study our marriage.

SHALI. I'd love to hear that poem again. What was it called?

YASIN. And since we're not going out –

SHALI. It had a lovely title.

YASIN. You can take off your coat.

SHALI. I'm cold, actually.

YASIN. But it's so warm.

SHALI. Not for me.

YASIN. There's an extra blanket in the closet.

SHALI. I don't mind being cold.

YASIN. Yes, but –

SHALI. Please don't ask me to take it off.

It won't get in the way.

YASIN. Shali, the mysteries between men and women have never included –

SHALI. *(overlapping)* Please don't.

YASIN. A coat.

SHALI. I'm not saying I won't do what you want. I'm just saying I'd prefer not to remove it while I'm doing it. It's not necessary, Yasin.

YASIN. A coat?

SHALI. I promise you it's not.

YASIN. I didn't marry you to lie next to a coat.

SHALI. I'll still be inside it.

YASIN. Who could tell?

SHALI. You could.

YASIN. If I turned down the lights would that make you more comfortable?

SHALI. It's not necessary, Yasin.

(*Lights up on* **HAMA**, *his first wife.*)

HAMA. It isn't. It's not necessary.

(*Lights down on hotel room.* **YASIN** *remembers a conversation with* **HAMA** *in their home years ago.*)

YASIN. I'm asking for something so little.

HAMA. And I have to be at work at eleven.

YASIN. That leaves you all morning.

HAMA. Why don't you go?

YASIN. Because I have a meeting about Cairo that's been on my calendar for a month.

HAMA. Can't you go tomorrow?

YASIN. I need the book today.

HAMA. What difference will one day make?

YASIN. I've only met this bookseller a week ago. He said he'd set the book aside until today. I said I would pick it up today.

HAMA. But it isn't necessary.

YASIN. It is.

HAMA. Can't you call and ask him for another day?

YASIN. He might think I don't have the money.

HAMA. We don't have the money.

YASIN. Yes, I know, but I need it. What if someone comes along and offers him more money for it?

HAMA. Is there a great demand for books about agricultural communities living on the Nineveh plain circa fourth century BC?

YASIN. I've been looking for this book for seven years.

HAMA. Where is this bookseller?

YASIN. In Bakir.

HAMA. Completely out of my way.

YASIN. *Please.*

HAMA. My aunt said Uday's men were in Bakir yesterday poking around.

YASIN. Wear your *hijab* then.

HAMA. I will not.

YASIN. Wear it in case they come back today.

HAMA. No.

YASIN. To be safe.

HAMA. Don't be silly, it isn't necessary.

YASIN. What then *is* necessary, Hama, if everything I ask of you is not?

HAMA. *You* are necessary.

YASIN. I am?

HAMA. Extremely necessary.

(They kiss.)

YASIN. I'll get your scarf.

HAMA. I've got everything in my bureau just so. I don't want your hands in there tearing it up.

YASIN. Then you get it.

HAMA. All right, I'll take it. But I won't wear it.

(She exits.)

(The memory fades.)

(Lights back up on the hotel room.)

YASIN. *(to* **SHALI***)* It isn't necessary.

SHALI. Thank you for understanding.

Think of the coat as a layer, a veil.

YASIN. Or perhaps I won't think of it at all.

*(***YASIN*** opens his suitcase. He removes a gift-wrapped box.)*

Your sister gave this to me.

SHALI. Do you know what it is?

YASIN. No. She only asked that I give it to you tonight.

(She opens the box and removes a deep green satin night-gown.)

SHALI. It's beautiful.

YASIN. You could try it on. See if it fits.

SHALI. I could try it later.

YASIN. Why not do it now?

>   *(beat)*

SHALI. If you like.

>   *(She is about to exit into the bathroom with it.)*

YASIN. Where are you going?

SHALI. To try it on.

YASIN. Shali?

SHALI. Yes?

YASIN. You'll come right out?

SHALI. *(not at all sure)* Yes, of course.

>   *(She exits into the bathroom.)*

>   *(Lights up on a room SHALI's home. Her younger sister MENA is there peeking through a keyhole. SHALI joins her. SHALI remembers their conversation.)*

MENA. What do you think?

SHALI. He's thin.

MENA. Thin is good. When they're thin they don't eat a lot. I used to toast almonds for Samir – kilos of them. Now I can't even look at an almond.

SHALI. His shirt is too big.

MENA. When you wash his clothes separate them from yours. He doesn't want your smell on him.

SHALI. He hunches over like he an old man.

MENA. It's probably his neck. Samir has terrible neck aches. I'm sure that's why he took a second wife. Her hands are big like a man's, but she can't cook or sew. She can't read or write either. That's why if you teach me to read he'll favor me again. Samir doesn't want a stupid wife. Now we're both dumb and interchangeable. I can cook, she can massage. But I will teach you to read Yasin's mind if you teach me to read the page.

(**SHALI** *peeks through the keyhole.*)

SHALI. Did you see his eyes? Very dark, deep set.

MENA. Looks mean nothing. When you clear the table, bring me his coffee cup so I can read the grounds.

SHALI. He doesn't smile much.

MENA. I like sad men.

(**MENA** *looks through the keyhole.*)

He looks very sad. I heard his wife died of cancer. You'll give him a child and he'll smile again. Put sage leaves and cardamon pods under your pillow when you make love so you'll have a boy. And whenever you lie with him close your eyes. It makes the time go faster. Most important you must convince him that you think about him every waking hour and nothing else. But Shali, you can't get married until you teach me to read.

SHALI. What about Baba?

MENA. Baba knows you and Luma read.

SHALI. Yes, and he doesn't like it.

MENA. I don't care, I want to learn. I know two more women who want to learn from you.

SHALI. I'm not a teacher.

MENA. They would pay you.

SHALI. And I'm not a merchant.

MENA. What should I tell them? They're desperate to read.

SHALI. If they come for tea with you tomorrow, I have no choice but to invite them in.

MENA. You'll like them. They're smart like you.

SHALI. If they were smart like me I wouldn't have to teach them.

(**MENA** *looks through the keyhole again.*)

MENA. Your man is smiling.

SHALI. No.

MENA. Look for yourself.

(**SHALI** *looks through the keyhole.*)

SHALI. That is not a smile.

MENA. It's a grin.

SHALI. I don't think I like him.

MENA. Baba likes him.

SHALI. He looks morbid.

MENA. Mama says all men are morbid.

(beat)

SHALI. No, I don't think he's for me.

MENA. Promise me you'll teach me to read before you marry.

SHALI. I don't think I'm going to marry him.

MENA. Promise me.

SHALI. Yes, yes, I'll do it. I promise. Now tell me what they're doing.

*(**MENA** looks through the keyhole.)*

MENA. The men are done. Go clear their cups.

SHALI. I doubt that I will ever like him.

MENA. And bring me the grounds!

*(**SHALI**'s memory fades. Lights down on the bathroom.)*

*(Lights up on the hotel room. **SHALI** enters.)*

SHALI. It looked quite nice. When we return home, I'll wear it to celebrate.

YASIN. I saw a coat like yours in a shop on Kings Street. There are all sorts of women's shops there. I can take you if you like.

SHALI. You have better things to spend your money on.

YASIN. You'd like this store.

SHALI. I'd like it better if it were in Mosul.

YASIN. If it were in Mosul you couldn't see through the windows. They'd be boarded up.

SHALI. The boards will come down and the doors will open.

YASIN. And what will be left inside?

SHALI. Everything will be exactly as it was. You believe it too, you must. If you were so concerned, you wouldn't have left.

YASIN. Maybe I left because I'm so concerned.

SHALI. But the Americans –

YASIN. *(overlapping)* We're not sure what the Americans are planning. Things disappear in war; objects in museums vanish.

SHALI. You care so much for these objects. What about the people?

YASIN. The objects are part of the people. They're the deepest, hidden, most secret part. They're the best part and the most important part to protect.

SHALI. You're talking about love.

YASIN. Yes, I love them. I do.

SHALI. And your statue, the one you care so much about, did you send it to Baghdad?

YASIN. We sent a great many –

SHALI. *(overlapping)* You said a great many people were concerned about it.

YASIN. We're concerned about every artifact.

SHALI. But you said it was special.

YASIN. They're all –

SHALI. *(overlapping)* Special to you.

YASIN. Yes.

SHALI. Is that your secret?

(beat)

YASIN. The statue of Inana had to be protected in a certain way.

SHALI. Different from the others?

YASIN. Yes.

SHALI. Why?

MOHAMMED *(offstage)* Yasin! Come quickly!

(Only YASIN hears him.)

YASIN. I'm not a superstitious man by nature. I never
    believed those stories we were taught as children. But
    when I saw the inscription –

MOHAMMED *(offstage)* Yasin please!

YASIN. There is an inscription on Inana's back that is very
    specific. You'd probably think it's a silly thing but I
    couldn't bring myself to pass judgement. You probably
    don't believe in such things as curses –

SHALI. *(overlapping)* I do believe in them.

YASIN. There was a curse carved on Inana's torso saying
    that if she were destroyed, or mutilated in any way,
    there would be terrible destruction throughout the
    land.

SHALI. Dear God.

YASIN. The only other statue of Inana was destroyed 800
    years ago on the first day of the Mongol invasion. The
    Mongols had threatened to sack Baghdad but no one
    believed them. They took Inana and the city fell. The
    Mongols slaughtered every living being in the city.
    Nothing was spared: not a child not a tree. Nothing
    living in Baghdad ever breathed again. And this statue
    of Inana, the one in the museum is the last one left.
    All the others are gone.

SHALI. So if someone came and took her, the Americans
    for example –

YASIN. *(overlapping)* Or anyone. People were coming in and
    out while we were packing.

SHALI. But you protected the statue.

    (He does not respond.)

    Tell me she is safe, Yasin. Tell me you guarded her with
    your very life and she is somewhere no one can touch
    her.

    (Lights down on hotel room.)

    *(****MOHAMMED**** enters.)*

    (Lights up on the courtyard of the Mosul Museum.)

(**YASIN** *remembers a conversation with him.*)

MOHAMMED. The goddess is gone.

YASIN. Gone?

MOHAMMED. I'd brought in my last blanket and I'd gone upstairs to wrap her –

YASIN. *(overlapping)* Are you sure?

MOHAMMED. Quite sure.

YASIN. Perhaps someone moved her.

MOHAMMED. I'm certain of it. The statue is missing. I'm so sorry Yasin.

YASIN. Dear God it's unbelievable.

MOHAMMED. I'm so sorry.

YASIN. Did you see anyone strange, a visitor, anyone at all near her?

MOHAMMED. No. No one.

YASIN. But this is terrible.

MOHAMMED. I'll call the police.

YASIN. The police? If the National finds out we've lost her, we'll never get her back. Even if she's found, they'll claim we can't protect her.

MOHAMMED. The truck to Baghdad is waiting. The driver says if he doesn't leave now –

YASIN. *(overlapping)* What if we give the driver Inana's crate and tell him to go with it.

MOHAMMED. It'll be too light.

YASIN. Then fill it with something.

MOHAMMED. Books?

YASIN. You'd need too many.

MOHAMMED. Wood?

YASIN. Too much noise.

MOHAMMED. There are some loose bricks in the courtyard. We'd only need a few. Do you really think we should be – ?

YASIN. *(overlapping)* Mohammed, if you aren't capable of stepping into a situation –

MOHAMMED. *(overlapping)* I am, yes – of course I am. I'll take care of it. But what happens when they open the crate and the statue isn't inside?

YASIN. It'll be months before they open it.

MOHAMMED. So what then?

YASIN. Miracles happen.

MOHAMMED. Thanks be to God.

YASIN. God is good. Was my Babylon tablet put on the truck?

MOHAMMED. Yes, Yasin, I gave it to the driver myself.

YASIN. Good. Now go fill Inana's crate and give it to the driver.

MOHAMMED. Do you think the statue's gone for good?

YASIN. Forever, you mean? I pray to God no.

MOHAMMED. God is merciful. She'll come back to us.

YASIN. Go! And Mohammed?

MOHAMMED. Yes?

YASIN. Not a word to anyone.

MOHAMMED. Not a word.

> (**MOHAMMED** *exits.*)
>
> *(Lights down on the museum.)*
>
> *(Lights back up on the hotel room.)*

SHALI. Yasin, what happened to the statue?

YASIN. Gone.

SHALI. Dear God.

YASIN. The museum was full of people packing cartons, we'd hired extra staff but –

SHALI. *(overlapping)* But God entrusted her to you.

YASIN. You don't understand.

SHALI. God gave her to you so that she would be protected.

YASIN. I did protect her!

SHALI. Our country is in terrible danger now. Did you tell anyone about the curse?

(The phone rings.)

YASIN. No. I didn't want to create –

SHALI. I must warn them.

YASIN. Shali –

SHALI. They don't know what's coming. They'll all be destroyed.

(The phone rings.)

YASIN. Where are you going?

SHALI. I need to get home.

YASIN. You can't leave.

*(**SHALI** exits.)*

Shali wait!

(The phone rings.)

*(**YASIN** exits.)*

(The phone rings.)

(Lights fade to black.)

End of Act One

ACT TWO

(The hotel bedroom an hour later. YASIN *is cutting out paper stars, five point stars. It is busy work for him.)*

(Lights up on the studio of EMAD AL-BAYIT. YASIN *enters the space where he works.)*

*(*YASIN *remembers a conversation with* EMAD*.)*

EMAD. I must apologize for the mess. I've been working on a terra cotta plaque. I haven't gotten the dragon quite right and it was supposed to be finished last week.

YASIN. I won't keep you.

EMAD. On the contrary, it's an honor to have you here.

YASIN. Then you know who I am?

EMAD. You're the curator. You're a friend of Abdel-Hakim Taliq.

YASIN. For many years.

EMAD. I shall miss his collection when it's gone to Tehran.

YASIN. I think he's wise.

EMAD. I don't know if he's wise but he's very careful with his treasures. Very protective. No doubt like you.

YASIN. Yes.

EMAD. Yes.

(a beat of awkward silence)

YASIN. Is there somewhere we can speak without being interrupted?

EMAD. No one comes around here. Too much dust.

YASIN. You have a reputation for making objects that are so beautiful we see them in museums all over the world.

EMAD. But not in yours.

YASIN. No.

EMAD. You hope.

YASIN. I'm quite positive.

EMAD. You have the Waru urn don't you?

YASIN. On the first floor, yes.

EMAD. *(slyly)* It's a lovely piece, isn't it?

(silence)

YASIN. Some would think you mean to tease us.

EMAD. Not at all. My vessels and vases are at best minor works of art inspired by the greatest antiquities. They aren't copies. Anyone familiar with the original would know that. They couldn't be for a thousand reasons. They're merely interpretations.

YASIN. Then how is it they wind up on display in so many venerated institutions?

EMAD. I don't keep track of what I sell. Once it leaves here I have nothing to do with it. If people misunderstand my handiwork and think it's valuable, if they say it's come from an Egyptian excavation or Syrian temple, I can't do anything about that.

YASIN. You don't like museums.

EMAD. Everything is so neat and orderly entombed in those glass cases. Who comes to your museum? Not the people in the neighborhood.

YASIN. They're welcome to.

EMAD. They're not your kind of people and they know it. You mock them. You put their history behind glass and then you ask them to pay to see it.

YASIN. If we didn't house the objects, we couldn't study them.

EMAD. Can't we just say they're beautiful and be done with it?

YASIN. Beauty itself means nothing. It needs to be put into historical context.

EMAD. Why not let them exist on their own, as objects here and now?

YASIN. If you don't believe in history, why copy an antiquity?

EMAD. Because I'm not that talented and they're far better than anything I could think up.

YASIN. You're an antiquarian at heart with a modernist viewpoint.

EMAD. My wife says my biggest problem is that I was born 3000 years too late.

(**EMAD** *has taken a pair of scissors and paper into his hands. He is cutting out shapes.*)

YASIN. What are you making there?

EMAD. My wife calls it my busy work. Years ago we went to Paris and saw Matisse's paper cuts. I loved them; they're the only contemporary art I like. I'm not very good at the execution, but I'm not paid to be. My fingers need to move so I give them paper and scissors and voilà, something happens. You fold here, cut there. I try not to get too involved in the mechanics. If I think of a bird while I cut, quite soon there's a sparrow sitting in my palm. Or something that resembles a sparrow. Here.

(*He hands* **YASIN** *the paper and scissors.*)

YASIN. I'm clumsy at this sort of thing.

EMAD. Even my wife can do it.

YASIN. I wouldn't know where to begin.

EMAD. Think of an object, the lines it has, the soft spots, the way it looks from a particular angle. Don't close your eyes, you'll poke yourself and bleed. I've done it.

(**YASIN** *tries but gives up.*)

YASIN. Nothing's coming.

EMAD. Try it again. Try it in that office of yours only make sure the door's closed.

YASIN. You've been to the museum?

EMAD. Many times.

YASIN. Are you familiar with the statue of Inana?

EMAD. Yes, of course. I've studied her at length. Oh, don't worry, I haven't done anything based on her. Yet.

YASIN. I've been instructed to make a copy of her. In this case you'd be authorized to do so.

EMAD. By whom?

YASIN. By me. I assure you it would be completely legal. The copy of the statue would be displayed and we'd keep the original in the main vault.

EMAD. And you'd be fooling people into thinking she was the original.

YASIN. We don't want to deprive the public from seeing her, however, we don't want her at risk either.

EMAD. Why now? Because of the Americans?

YASIN. I've been thinking about doing this since the Gulf War. We haven't lost her yet. I don't want this to be the time our luck runs out. Do I have your attention yet?

EMAD. Very much so.

YASIN. Shall we move on to more mundane subjects then?

EMAD. Money?

YASIN. And time.

EMAD. A job like that would take approximately six months to execute providing I agreed to do it.

YASIN. I'd need it sooner.

EMAD. As I mentioned to you before, I'm already behind. I have another commission due in less than three months and another one after that. But if you're prepared to wait a year –

YASIN. *(cutting him short)* I'm not.

EMAD. Then I'm afraid I can't help you. I can recommend someone to you in Rome. He's excellent.

YASIN. It has to be you and it has to be done as soon as possible.

EMAD. I've been known to make special arrangements.

YASIN. What if your schedule was clear and you could put all your resources behind it?

EMAD. You mean in a perfect world?

YASIN. Yes.

EMAD. I could have it to you in eight weeks. But as I told you –

YASIN. *(overlapping)* My benefactor has very deep pockets.

(beat)

EMAD. Four million dinars.

YASIN. *(shocked)* Four million?

EMAD. For the statue of Inana in eight weeks time, yes, four million dinars.

YASIN. Is that number negotiable?

EMAD. Not at all.

YASIN. Four million?

EMAD. Dinars.

YASIN. I don't have anywhere near that much.

EMAD. Then I'm afraid I can't help you.

YASIN. Is there some other arrangement we could make?

EMAD. Such as?

YASIN. We're both creative men.

(beat)

EMAD. Then let us both think on it another night.

YASIN. I have little time to waste dwelling on the impossible.

EMAD. I assure you it's not the impossible I seek.
Perhaps there's something else you can give me, something with a value greater than money.

YASIN. It would have to be something extraordinary.

EMAD. I was thinking the same thing.

*(Lights down on **EMAD**.)*

(Lights up on the hotel room.)

*(Someone knocks at the door. **YASIN** opens it and **SHALI** enters.)*

YASIN. I almost called the police.

SHALI. Why didn't you?

YASIN. I wanted to give you more time.

(silence)

I didn't think you'd go far.

SHALI. I was in the stairwell.

(silence)

YASIN. I unpacked your things. They're in that chest. I cleaned the drawers thoroughly before I put your clothing in. We'll have to call housekeeping for more towels.

SHALI. I wanted to go to the airport, but I had no ticket. I couldn't buy a ticket because I had no money.

YASIN. I can give you some.

SHALI. I've come back.

YASIN. In case you want to leave.

SHALI. Are you still going out tomorrow?

YASIN. I have to.

SHALI. Did you get your phone call then?

YASIN. When you left? That was the waiter calling about the tray.

SHALI. When I call my father tomorrow may I tell him about the statue of Inana? That it was stolen?

YASIN. No.

SHALI. Please, Yasin. They don't know.

YASIN. They don't need to know.

SHALI. But the story you told me –

YASIN. *(overlapping)* Wasn't finished. You ran out before I was through. You overreacted my dear. The statue was returned.

SHALI. Returned to you?

YASIN. To the museum.

SHALI. Do you know who took it?

YASIN. The guards. It's a terrible assumption to make –

SHALI. *(overlapping)* But under the circumstances –

YASIN. *(overlapping)* It seemed reasonable. We'd hired extra men for protection but I didn't know them all. So as head of the museum I began my investigation. We didn't want to alarm anyone and we didn't want word to get out that we'd sent bricks to Baghdad.

SHALI. Of course.

YASIN. A day later I heard from her kidnappers that she was safe. She was in excellent shape, she hadn't been harmed, and eventually she was returned.

SHALI. She came back?

YASIN. Thanks be to God yes.

SHALI. How long was she gone?

YASIN. Eight weeks, give or take a few days. They kept saying it was imminent, then they'd call and say no and leave us hanging and we kept waiting.

SHALI. Did you call the police?

YASIN. No, no. They told us if we did, we'd never see the statue again.

SHALI. How much did you pay?

YASIN. Not a dinar.

SHALI. Incredible.

YASIN. An authentic miracle.

SHALI. Where is it now?

YASIN. In a storage space in the National Museum.

SHALI. You sent her to the ones who wanted to keep her?

YASIN. I sent her to a steel lined vault where I knew she'd be safe and protected.

SHALI. I didn't think you'd send her. Not for all the world.

YASIN. It was what they were all expecting.

SHALI. Thanks be to God no one found out she was missing or you'd have been in trouble.

(beat)

Who found the statue?

YASIN. I did. The men left it inside the gates.

SHALI. The locked gates?

YASIN. Yes.

SHALI. So they had a key?

YASIN. Which points to the guards once again. We've changed all the museum locks.

SHALI. And nothing else was taken?

YASIN. Thank God, no.

SHALI. What are you doing?

YASIN. I'm getting ready for bed.

SHALI. I'm still interested in your story.

YASIN. The story's over.

SHALI. What about – ?

YASIN. It's been a very long day. We can continue tomorrow, if you like, when I've returned from my meeting.

SHALI. You haven't received your phone call.

YASIN. I'm sure they'll call in the morning.

SHALI. You said tonight.

YASIN. Good night, Shali.

(*But* **SHALI** *isn't finished.*)

SHALI. Before you go to bed, you might as well know I'm not 18 and I'm not 23. I'm 30.

YASIN. Thirty!

SHALI. Actually I'm 32. Does it matter?

YASIN. I don't know, my head is spinning from the arithmetic.

SHALI. You told my father you wanted a literate woman of some independence.

YASIN. That's right. Modest and yet independent.

SHALI. I think I've shown you my modesty.

YASIN. To a fault, yes. As for your independence, again your father lied. According to you, you've never spent a single moment alone in a room.

SHALI. We come from a small village, my cousins are like my brothers, my sisters are my twin selves. I don't leave the house unless it's with my father, and he seldom has time to waste on me. But I read and I write and I think. I have opinions and ideas though no one's heard them. The tiger may be in a cage, but if you ask him if he's independent, he'll tell you yes. Yasin, you can come and go as you please in Mosul, but are you truly independent? Can you travel to the cities you want, meet the people you want, read the books you want, in short do everything you want to illuminate your work?

YASIN. No, of course not.

SHALI. Then what makes you independent?

(Lights down on the hotel room.)

*(Lights up on **DOMINIC CROFT**, an enthusiastic curator in the Department of the Ancient Near East at the British Museum.)*

*(**YASIN** remembers a telephone conversation with him months ago.)*

YASIN. We aren't allowed to move freely in and out of the country anymore. Saddam doesn't want anybody leaving especially now. So the Travel Ministry has cracked down on everyone even on people like me.

DOMINIC. Can't you just say you're taking a research trip?

YASIN. They'll say it's not a good enough reason. Believe me Dominic, I want to come.

DOMINIC. I think we'd be awfully lucky to have you at the museum. I know we haven't met, but McGuire Gibson's an old friend of mine and he speaks so highly of you. Your experience in the trenches would be invaluable to us. The first thing I'd do is put you into a lecture series. You'd be a big draw in light of what's going on at the U.N. The whole notion of your country having WMDs is absurd. Don't you think?

YASIN. Pardon?

DOMINIC. WMDs in Iraq – you don't have any do you?

YASIN. Not at the museum, no.

DOMINIC. None of us are backing the Americans. None of the real people here.

YASIN. Yes, we've been watching.

DOMINIC. Are you safe there?

YASIN. We're storing most everything in the National's vaults.

DOMINIC. I meant you. Might be a good time for you to get out then. Do you have family there?

YASIN. Most of my family went to Toronto in '91.

DOMINIC. Why didn't you?

YASIN. My wife wanted to stay.

DOMINIC. You're married?

YASIN. She died some years ago.

DOMINIC. Oh, I'm so sorry.

(awkward pause)

It'd be a full position here. I'm sure I told you that. Benefits, vacation, everything but lunch money. The trouble is, I can't hold the job open indefinitely and there's several more people you need to meet. There must be some reason for you to come to London. Get back to me as soon as you can, Yasin. I'm still hoping we can make this work.

YASIN. Thank you Dominic.

DOMINIC. See you then.

*(Lights down on **DOMINIC**.)*

(Lights back on up on the hotel room.)

SHALI. Yasin?

(No response.)

SHALI. What are you going to do with me?

YASIN. Do with you?

SHALI. Husbands do things to wives.

YASIN. And wives do things to husbands.

SHALI. I've never been a wife before. Was your first wife a good wife? Were there things she did that you liked?

YASIN. Yes. Many things.

SHALI. If there's anything you remember that you want me to do, will you tell me?

(silence)

YASIN. She was also 32. She worked in Al Salam Hospital. She took the histories of people who came for treatment. She was the last woman in her department.

SHALI. Was she ill for a long time?

YASIN. Ill?

SHALI. My sister said she had cancer.

YASIN. Who told her that?

SHALI. I didn't ask.

YASIN. She was taken.

SHALI. Oh God.

YASIN. She had gone to Bakir to pick up a book for me. Uday Hussein saw her on the street. She attracted his attention because she wasn't wearing her *hijab.* You see, Hama was very beautiful. She made men stare. Even the imams couldn't help it. When she didn't come home I went to the police station. They laughed at me. Then they told me not to make trouble. One of them took pity on me. He told me that Uday would never let Hama come home. They would take her to the desert to die. So I went to the desert every night to watch for the trucks but they never stopped at the same place twice. The desert is so big. She could be anywhere. After two years I gave up looking.

SHALI. I'm so sorry.

YASIN. "Cancer" is an interesting word for Uday, but I don't think that was what your sister had in mind.

(pause)

You're so anxious to go back to Iraq, let me see if I can get you on a flight.

SHALI. Yasin –

YASIN. Maybe there's one to Amman in the morning. You can take a cab to the airport. You have money now.

SHALI. Wait a minute –

YASIN. *(overlapping)* Call your father and tell him he can pick you up there.

SHALI. I can't go back alone.

YASIN. Tell them I beat you. Tell them I died. A widow on your honeymoon.

SHALI. They'd never believe me.

YASIN. That's your problem.

SHALI. Why are you doing this to me?

YASIN. I did not want a wife! I told you before, I was not looking for you or anybody else to marry.

SHALI. Then why am I here?

(She exits to the bathroom.)

YASIN. I made a mistake.

(Lights up on **EMAD** *in his workroom.* **YASIN** *enters the workroom. He remembers their conversation.)*

EMAD. The problem is that you want something from me that you can't afford. It's a dilemma, isn't it? How do you satisfy a craving for something completely beyond your reach? You can kill it so it's out of your mind. That often works.

YASIN. Not in this case.

EMAD. Or you can bend things to fit, turn the pieces until they fall into place. I've given it some thought and I've discovered there is something you can give me. Something with a value greater than money.

YASIN. I can't give you anything from the museum.

EMAD. That wasn't what I had in mind.

YASIN. What is it then?

EMAD. I want you.

YASIN. Me?

EMAD. Our friend Abdel-Hakim tells me that he's looking for a bride for you.

YASIN. Out of the goodness of his heart, but not at my request.

EMAD. I have the perfect girl. If you agree to marry her, I'll make you the statue within two months time for nothing at all. Money doesn't enter into it.

YASIN. Are you mad?

EMAD. Not at all.

YASIN. You want me to marry a girl in exchange for the statue?

EMAD. Not only marry her but leave the country with her as soon as possible.

YASIN. You are mad.

EMAD. Only delirious with joy. I have found a solution to both our problems.

YASIN. What is your problem?

EMAD. She is my daughter.

YASIN. Do you love her so little?

EMAD. On the contrary, I favor her above all my children, but she's too smart for her own good. She's talking about teaching women to read, groups of women in secret. Too dangerous. I want you to take her wherever you like and never come back.

YASIN. You can't be serious.

EMAD. If you return, I'll tell the world that I created a copy of the greatest statue in Iraq for your museum at your request.

YASIN. This isn't at all what I was thinking.

EMAD. It's a very creative idea. I'm so pleased with it, I'll even buy the travel tickets.

YASIN. What if I could come close to getting you the money you requested? What if I paid you over time?

EMAD. I don't want money. I like these terms much better.

YASIN. But they're impossible.

EMAD. Why?

YASIN. I don't know anything about your daughter.

EMAD. What kind of woman are you looking for?

YASIN. I'm not looking for a woman. I don't want to get married.

EMAD. Do you want to be alone for the rest of your life?

(*YASIN doesn't respond.*)

Then you must get married. This is the perfect opportunity for you, Yasin. You get a wife and your statue. In fact, I think you come out much better in the end than I do.

YASIN. How would it look for me to marry the daughter of the biggest art forger in the Middle East?

EMAD. A month before you wed, I'll announce that I'm giving up my business. I'll close the studio. That'll be my very public wedding gift to you both.

YASIN. You'd do that?

EMAD. When you have children you'll understand better. Besides, after I make your statue, how could I possibly follow that?

(*A phone rings off stage.*)

(*Lights down on* **EMAD**.)

(*Lights up on the London hotel room where the telephone is ringing.* **SHALI** *enters.*)

YASIN. (*answering the phone*) Hello?

(*Lights up on the front desk in the lobby. The* **WAITER** *is on the phone.*)

WAITER. Huzzah, Manchester!

YASIN. Yes?

WAITER. Sir, there's a man downstairs in the lobby asking for you. He says you're expecting him.

YASIN. Did he tell you his name?

WAITER. Says he won't give it out.

YASIN. May I speak to him?

WAITER. He won't come on the phone. He says he wants to come up.

YASIN. Yes, all right. Send him up.

WAITER. Do you want me to come with him? It's included in the hotel service fee. I don't mind sir, really.

YASIN. It isn't necessary. Thank you.

(Lights down on the **WAITER.** *)*

There's someone coming up.

SHALI. What time is it?

YASIN. I wasn't expecting him now.

SHALI. Do you know him?

YASIN. He's a friend of a friend.

SHALI. But not your friend?

YASIN. No. But it makes no difference.

SHALI. I have nothing to offer him. The biscuits and tea are gone.

YASIN. He's here to pick something up. He won't stay long.

SHALI. He'll think we're rude if we don't offer him something.

(They sit in silence until someone knocks on their door.)

YASIN. Hello?

MESSENGER. *(offstage)* Yasin Shalid, yes?

*(***YASIN*** opens the door and the* **MESSENGER** *enters. He is on his cell phone.)*

YASIN. They said you'd come tomorrow.

MESSENGER. *(into phone)* It's him. He's here.

YASIN. Do you have a word for me? A password?

MESSENGER. *(into phone)* He's asking for a password. I can't hear you, speak up. Yes, he's here. Well, then ask Saeed if he knows.

(to **YASIN** *)*

I apologize.

(into phone)

Yes, I'm here.

YASIN. What is going on?

MESSENGER. *(to* **YASIN***)* Omar usually does the collection but he's trying to get back for the burial.

SHALI. *(to* **YASIN***)* Do you know what he's talking about?

MESSENGER. *(into phone)* Then ask Baba. I don't care, call him.

YASIN. I need the password.

MESSENGER. *(into phone)* Then get it from –

YASIN. That was the plan.

MESSENGER. *(to* **YASIN***)* John Curtis.

YASIN. That's it. Good.

SHALI. *(to* **YASIN***)* Who is John Curtis?

YASIN. That's the password.

MESSENGER. Was he a friend of Abdel-Hakim Taliq?

YASIN. No.

MESSENGER. Were you a friend?

YASIN. Yes, of course I know him. That's why you're here.

MESSENGER. There was a fire in the bookshop yesterday. They burned it all down.

YASIN. Yesterday?

SHALI. Dear God.

MESSENGER. *(into phone)* No, I don't have it yet.

YASIN. What about Abdel-Hakim?

MESSENGER. He's gone. It spread down the block, five more died. I don't know if Omar will make it back in time. Abdel-Hakim was his uncle.

YASIN. How'd it start?

MESSENGER. Like most fires.

SHALI. How?

MESSENGER. Somebody said something.

(pause)

Where's the package?

SHALI. I'm sorry for your loss.

MESSENGER. Where's the thing that brought me?

YASIN. It's over here.

(He points to the large red suitcase.)

MESSENGER. *(into phone)* Tell Saeed I've got it.

SHALI. *(off the suitcase)* You're taking that?

MESSENGER. The plan's still the same on our end. God willing it's still going where it's expected.

YASIN. I'll give you a hand.

*(The **MESSENGER** and **YASIN** heft the suitcase.)*

SHALI. Where're you going?

MESSENGER. *(into phone)* We're coming down now.

SHALI. Yasin –

MESSENGER. *(into phone)* Bring the car around front.

YASIN. *(to **SHALI**)* Lock the door.

SHALI. Wait –

YASIN. If the phone rings, if a man calls looking for me, tell him I'll only be gone for a minute. If you think of it, get a telephone number where he can be reached.

(They exit with the suitcase.)

*(**SHALI** looks around the room. She opens a small suitcase and rummages around until she finds an orange.)*

*(Lights up on **EMAD**. **SHALI** remembers a conversation with her father nearly twenty years ago. She gives him the orange to peel.)*

EMAD. The story of The One Handed Man.

SHALI. Yes, Baba.

EMAD. Installment 34.

SHALI. Go on. Please.

EMAD. The One-Handed Man had sailed to Persia and now he was face to face at last with –

SHALI. *(overlapping)* Karimma gave me that orange and Mama one, too. She said it was because I'm a good girl.

EMAD. My Shali's a very good girl.

SHALI. And Saddam knows that, right Baba? Saddam knows I'm good.

EMAD. Yes, my love.

SHALI. I've been good for how many days now?

EMAD. Four days.

SHALI. Only four?

EMAD. Four is a good number. Last week you were only good for two days.

SHALI. So, I'm improving.

EMAD. Yes, Shali.

SHALI. And Saddam knows that, right Baba?

EMAD. Saddam loves my Shali.

SHALI. And I love this orange.

EMAD. It's a very good orange.

SHALI. How many colors of orange are there in the world?

EMAD. Fifty-two.

SHALI. Imagine.

EMAD. Exactly fifty two.

SHALI. Is there more orange or blue?

EMAD. There are only forty colors of blue.

SHALI. And twenty-nine yellows.

EMAD. Thirty.

SHALI. Thirty?

EMAD. I found another one yesterday.

SHALI. Where was it?

EMAD. Hiding under the chair.

SHALI. Was it frightened?

EMAD. This yellow was not.

SHALI. It was bold, then?

EMAD. Quite bold.

SHALI. *(marveling)* Thirty yellows.

EMAD. *(testing her)* And how many reds?

SHALI. Ninety-two.

EMAD. Ninety-two reds.

SHALI. Does Saddam know there are ninety-two reds?

EMAD. Oh, I'm sure he does.

SHALI. Saddam knows everything, right, Baba?

EMAD. Yes, my daughter.

SHALI. Saddam knows I'm a good girl and that I'll be good for much more than four days. I'll be good for four hundred days! Four thousand days! Four million days!

(pause)

And then...

EMAD. And then.

(Lights down on EMAD.)

(SHALI finishes the orange.)

(Lights down on the hotel room.)

(Lights up on ABDEL-HAKIM. in his bookshop in Bakir. YASIN enters. He remembers a conversation with ABDEL-HAKIM who has a fresh black eye.)

ABDEL-HAKIM. They broke my nose.

YASIN. You should close.

ABDEL-HAKIM. That's what they want.

YASIN. Look, at you, you're *eroding.*

ABDEL-HAKIM. I'm not.

YASIN. They're taking you apart bit by bit. They're not going to give up. They want you out. They'll just keep coming at you.

ABDEL-HAKIM. "When sorrows come, they come not single spies, But in battalions!"

YASIN. What can you do, you're one man.

ABDEL-HAKIM. Is that what you say when you look in the mirror?

YASIN. I try not to look.

ABDEL-HAKIM. I have the picture I promised of my cousin's daughter. I don't think she looks in the mirror either.

YASIN. I thank you for your generosity, but it seems I've already found a bride. Her father's a customer of yours.

ABDEL-HAKIM. Tell me who.

YASIN. Emad Al-Bayit.

ABDEL-HAKIM. The forger?

YASIN. The artist.

ABDEL-HAKIM. He's to be your father-in-law?

YASIN. Life is strange and authentic in it's miracles.

ABDEL-HAKIM. "Keep your friends close, but your enemies closer."

YASIN. He's my enemy no more.

ABDEL-HAKIM. God is greatest. I wish you joy beyond measure.

YASIN. Do you know his daughter Shali?

ABDEL-HAKIM. I know nothing about his family. He keeps them out in the country.

YASIN. Shali and I are going on a wedding trip after we're married. We're going to London. Do you know people there?

ABDEL-HAKIM. A few booksellers from the old days.

YASIN. The travel ministry's allowing one suitcase for Shali and one for me, plus two suitcases for my work. I'll give you access to one of those, but the books must relate to art or antiquities. They must look like books that might belong to me.

ABDEL-HAKIM. I have hundreds of books like those.

YASIN. Hundreds I cannot take. Pick twenty and call your friends. See if they can get them to Tehran for you. We leave February fourth.

ABDEL-HAKIM. Thank you my friend. A hundred blessings on your marriage! A thousand blessings on you both!

YASIN. I'll return in a few days.

ABDEL-HAKIM. Yasin, what can I do to repay you? Anything. Name it.

YASIN. *(gently)* Close the shop.

*(Lights down on **ABDEL-HAKIM**.)*

*(**YASIN** enters the hotel room. **SHALI** is waiting for him.)*

Did anyone ring?

SHALI. No, no one.

YASIN. Were you here the whole time?

SHALI. Yes, Yasin, I was alone for twelve minutes.

YASIN. And nobody rang?

SHALI. Did you hear that, Yasin? I was alone!

YASIN. I'm sorry to have you left you so long.

SHALI. I'm sorry your friend died.

YASIN. He was creating a library in Tehran. He'd been able to get sixteen thousand books out before the fire. They said he knew his time was coming, so he'd doubled and tripled his efforts.

SHALI. There were books in the suitcase?

YASIN. The first Arabic translation of Isaiah with illuminated pages, six books of drawings that date before the Ottoman Empire, twelve books by Wamidh Mohammed, an alphabet illustrated by the painter Omar Kirtani – all one-of-a-kind books found nowhere else. Not even in the British Museum.

(pause)

What if the British have changed their minds? What if they don't want to meet with me?

SHALI. Why wouldn't they?

YASIN. I am nothing compared to the people who work there. I have neither the experience nor the degrees.

SHALI. You have worked in Babylon and Nineveh. You're the chief of the second largest museum –

YASIN. *(overlapping)* These people have traveled all over the world.

SHALI. But you've lived and worked in the cradle of civilization. Can they say that?

YASIN. There's another department of Near East studies at the Victoria and Albert Museum. Perhaps tomorrow I could call over there.

SHALI. Why do you need to see another?

YASIN. There are probably teaching posts where I could be useful.

SHALI. You mean work? Here?

YASIN. The meeting tomorrow was about –

SHALI. *(overlapping)* But if you really don't believe the British Museum will call, there's no reason to stay. You don't need to find another –

YASIN. Shali.

SHALI. We can leave tomorrow.

YASIN. Shali, you must know.

SHALI. I don't know anything except that I'm looking forward to going home.

YASIN. We are home.

(silence)

SHALI. I'll go without you. I'll leave tomorrow.

YASIN. Don't go.

SHALI. Where's my ticket? My return ticket.

(He doesn't respond.)

Please tell me where it is. I beg you.

YASIN. I can't.

SHALI. I just want to see it. I won't touch it.

YASIN. I'm sorry.

SHALI. I beg you please.

YASIN. There is no return ticket.

(silence)

SHALI. No one knows where I am.

YASIN. Your father knows.

(silence)

SHALI. I'm sure he didn't want me to go.

YASIN. He understood that you're my wife now.

(She suddenly panics.)

SHALI. I have to go home.

YASIN. Shali –

SHALI. I need to go home now.

(She wildly throws clothes in suitcases.)

YASIN. We are staying here.

SHALI. I'm not staying in this dirty hotel room with filthy plates and disgusting tea and people in the airport that stare at me. I demand to go home. I demand that you take me there. NOW!

YASIN. I can't help you, I'm sorry.

SHALI. My sister Mena – I didn't finish – I promised her I wouldn't leave until she'd learned everything. She doesn't know it all. She has to learn. She has to LEARN. SHE HAS TO LEARN!

(He embraces her and then steps back to look at her.)

SHALI. Why did you – ?

YASIN. What is that in your – ?

SHALI. You can't run at me like that.

YASIN. I'm sorry.

SHALI. Certain things still need to be explained.

YASIN. What is that?

SHALI. What is it I have there? Something hard, where it should be soft? Something empty where it should be full? You're asking about my left arm. Or what should be my left arm. Would you like to see it?

YASIN. I don't –

SHALI. Shall I take off the coat now?

YASIN. Did I – ?

SHALI. You haven't done anything. Do you want me to remove my coat, yes or no?

YASIN. Yes.

(She takes off her coat. Her left arm is missing below the shoulder. She wears a prosthetic device inside her white satin glove.)

SHALI. So you understand why we have to go back. The rest of me is still there in the hospital outside of Samarra. In the refrigerators. We have to go.

YASIN. They said that to protect you.

SHALI. No, it's true. My father told me –

YASIN. *(overlapping)* Your father created the lie.

SHALI. His friend worked there. He showed me pictures.

YASIN. He lied to comfort you.

SHALI. I think you're the liar.

YASIN. I swear to you, there is no hospital.

SHALI. Liar!

YASIN. Shali, my love –

SHALI. LIAR! You just want to keep me here! For what?

YASIN. To be my wife!

SHALI. How can I be your wife if I only have one arm?

YASIN. You could have no arms and be my wife!

　　(silence)

SHALI. I saw it in my father's workroom. It was for you, wasn't it? We hadn't seen my father for weeks. My brother said it would be his greatest achievement. I peeked inside once in the middle of the night. The light was out and I had my...I had my flashlight with me. I saw her by the light of the little flashlight I brought. I would look inside his work room late at night. It was the only way I could see what he was doing and feel some connection to him still. There was a statue of a woman without an arm. Was it Inana?

YASIN. It was.

SHALI. So you bought two statues. You were better off keeping the stone one. She's worth more.

YASIN. Not to me.

SHALI. You don't seem like the kind of man who would traffic in forgeries.

YASIN. You don't seem like the kind of woman who'd believe in imaginary hospitals.

SHALI. What ten year-old girl calls her father a liar? I wanted to believe it as much for him as for me. I wanted to be such a good girl.

There were two of me. The one before and the one after. I always wanted to be the other Shali. We all yearn for the other self, the one that is connected somehow to our childhood and then is pried from our memory by time until finally we are forced to let it go. I didn't realize it was so until I stood here with you. I don't want her back now. Really, I don't.

You are the first person in my life to tell me the truth.

(pause)

I'm hungry.

(He rummages through his suitcase and pulls out a bag of dates. She finds another orange in her bag.)

YASIN. I can never return to Mosul. There are things I've done.

SHALI. *(teasing him)* Evil things?

YASIN. Yes, very evil.

SHALI. Oooh hooo.

YASIN. But very necessary.

SHALI. Will you tell me what you did?

YASIN. I've sworn an oath not to tell.

SHALI. I will swear the same. Who else knows the secret?

YASIN. No one.

SHALI. *(delighted)* No one! Then it would just be us who knew?

YASIN. No one else.

SHALI. I swear if you tell me, I'll never tell another soul the evil thing you did, no matter what.

YASIN. *(teasing her)* Even if you are captured?

SHALI. Yes.

YASIN. And even if you are –

(He stops short.)

SHALI. And tortured, yes.

YASIN. I'm sorry.

SHALI. I wasn't tortured. They just cut it off. I don't remember everything that happened. Someone told me a man held me down.

I had been walking on the street with my father. We had gone to visit his cousin who lived in Basra. I remember there was an old garden set back from the street next to a house and inside the garden was a date tree. I was hungry and I wanted something to eat. I took the date and suddenly there was a man standing next to me screaming at me. He demanded I give it to him and I ate it instead. It was the most sweetly wonderful thing I had ever tasted. I remember my father was laughing so I reached for another one. The man grabbed me by the arm and dragged me into the house, this honey colored palace. There were women looking at me from one of the balconies. I don't remember the room. Even my father couldn't protect me. Even my father, who was such a big man, a large man, could not stop them. I was –

(The phone rings.)

Yasin?

YASIN. Finish your thought.

SHALI. *The phone.*

(The phone rings again.)

YASIN. You were going to say that even at the age of ten, you were too beautiful.

SHALI. Yasin answer the phone.

YASIN. Shali there's something I need to tell you.

SHALI. But it could be them.

(The phone rings again.)

YASIN. Listen to me –

SHALI. Yasin –

(The phone is silent.)

YASIN. I did not send the original statue to Baghdad.

SHALI. No, I didn't think so.

(YASIN picks up one of the suitcases as the hotel room transforms.)

(The lights change. Music.)

(YASIN and SHALI are in the desert near Nineveh, Iraq. There is a moon in the night sky.)

YASIN. I am a very bad liar.

SHALI. It's a quality to be admired in a man.

YASIN. I sent them your father's Inana, the copy.

SHALI. But they will think it's the original.

YASIN. Yes.

SHALI. My husband is a clever man.

(Lights fade up on two statues of Inana, the copy and the original.)

YASIN. The Temple of Ishtar is in Nineveh, in the middle of the widest plain. In 1853 Hamza Rassam found Inana there. Since then it's been excavated and studied many times for many years. Hundreds of antiquities have been found and spread throughout Iraq. And some black market thieves have taken them beyond. There's an underground vault in the temple twenty feet below ground. I discovered it years ago.

SHALI. You took her home.

YASIN. Yes.

SHALI. Where Ralwa could watch over her.

YASIN. Ralwa and Hama and Abdel-Hakim and Yusuf and the rest of the ghosts, there are hundreds of thousands of them. Let the living find her there in calmer generations.

SHALI. There will never be calmer generations. But she will be found again.

YASIN. God willing.

(Lights down on the two statues.)

(SHALI regards the heavens.)

SHALI. "A moon in a light blue sky."

YASIN. We are inside the poem.

SHALI. Or the poem is inside us.

(off the suitcase)

What did you bring?

YASIN. The museum.

SHALI. In your suitcase?

YASIN. When objects go missing during war, many are found but there's no evidence where they rightfully belong. Databases get destroyed. Computers go missing. If something ends up on a desk in Japan and we try to claim it belongs to us, we need proof. Inside is the proof.

(He opens the suitcase and shows her thousands of index cards stacked inside. He shuffles through a stack and hands her three.)

SHALI. *(reading)* "Small winged lion from the palace of Sargon the Second."

"Large clay pottery oven dated 4000 BC."

"Three cuneiform tablets from Khorsabad."

YASIN. There's also a copy of each on Mohammed's desk.

SHALI. "This marriage, this silence

fully mixed with spirit."

(He closes the suitcase.)

(They are bathed in the light of the moon.)

YASIN. You are standing here and I still don't know who you are, yet I feel closer to you than to anyone or anything I have ever known.

SHALI. I am 92 reds, 30 yellows, 52 oranges, and 40 blues. Yasin, my love, I am yours.

(Lights fade to black.)

The End

ABOUT THE PLAYWRIGHT

MICHELE LOWE is the recipient of the 2010 Francesca Primus Prize for her play *Inana* (Denver Center Theatre). She was also a finalist for both the 2010 Steinberg/ATCA New Play Award for her plays *Inana* and *Victoria Musica* (Cincinnati Playhouse in the Park), which marks the first time in the award's 33 year history that a playwright has been independently nominated for two plays in one season, and the 2009 Susan Smith Blackburn Prize for *Inana*. Her play *Map of Heaven* was developed at the Colorado New Play Summit and will also premiere in Denver in 2011.

Lowe is the author of *The Smell of the Kill* (Broadway debut), *String of Pearls* (Primary Stages; Outer Critics Circle Nomination for Outstanding Off-Broadway Play), *Backsliding in the Promised Land* (Syracuse Stage) and *Mezzulah, 1946* (City Theatre in Pittsburgh). She is the librettist and lyricist for the musical *A Thousand Words Come to Mind* (Zipper Theatre), which she wrote with composer Scott Richards. Lowe and Richards are currently working on a musical commission for Signature Theatre in Virginia.

Lowe has been commissioned by Denver Center Theatre, Cincinnati Playhouse, and Geva Theatre. Her plays have been produced by the Vineyard Theatre, Intiman Theatre, Florida Stage, Reykjavik City Theatre (Iceland), Berkshire Theatre Festival, and Asolo Repertory Theatre among dozens of others. Her work has been developed at the Williamstown Theatre Festival, Eugene O'Neill National Music Theater Conference, New Harmony Project, PlayLabs, New York Stage & Film, Hartford Stage's BRAND: NEW Festival, the ACT & Hedgebrook Women Playwrights Festival and the Lark Play Development Center. Her work appears in *New Playwrights/ The Best Plays of 2005* (Smith and Kraus, 2006), *The Best Women's Stage Monologues 2005* (Smith and Kraus, 2006) and *Monologues for Women by Women* (Heinemann, 2004). Lowe is a graduate of Northwestern University's Medill School of Journalism. She is a member of The Dramatists Guild and ASCAP.